The Inside Story

Living and Learning Through Life's Storms

By Donald G. Ryder, M.S.

Printed in the United States of America.

Published by: RYDER Publishing Company
                2805 E. Golden West Avenue
                Visalia, California 93292 U.S.A.

Library of Congress Cataloging-in-Publication Data

Ryder, Donald G., 1946-
    The Inside Story.

    Summary: A wise old tree shares with a young seedling the positive and negative experiences that have shaped his growth, bringing him the knowledge that the hardships in life create strength and love.
    [1. Trees—Fiction] I. Title.
PZ7.R97517In 1985   [Fic]   85-27780
ISBN 0-935973-38-9

 Printed on recycled paper

Dedicated to all those who never give up but rather keep on trying.

Also dedicated to Yvonne, Michelle, Kelly and Andrew.

A special thanks to Don Mullen for the illustrations.

"Why Am I Here?"

THE INSIDE STORY

Bantam......Foster......both quite common, and at the same time, both very special. Bantam is a very young tree, not much bigger than a seedling. Bantam is sensitive, and curious and wants to learn all about life. Foster is a very old tree who has had many experiences throughout life. In fact all that's left of him is a stump. But a very wise stump.

One beautiful summer day as Bantam and Foster were soaking up the warm rays of the sun, short little Bantam looked over at Foster and said, "Why am I here, Foster?"

Foster looked at Bantam and could tell that young Bantam was serious and was asking a deep, penetrating question. He paused for a moment and then replied, "You're here for the same reason that I am here, to grow into the best tree that you can be."

"Get To Know Yourself"

Bantam quickly quipped, "That's a tall order! So tell me, Foster, how do I grow?"

"Well Bantam, every year you form new wood just under your bark. Early in the spring you make large cells and you grow very fast. Later in the season you make smaller cells and you grow slower."

"How can I grow to be big, strong and wise?" asked Bantam.

"First of all you must get to know yourself," said Foster. "Listen to that silent voice guiding you from within. Know what kind of tree you are and then don't try to be some other tree. Think well of yourself. Believe in yourself. Know your roots. Always grow toward the sun and you will stand tall and straight. And remember, everything that happens to you throughout your life is for a purpose. It all depends on your attitude."

"Take The Gift Of Life You Have, And Grow And Develop Yourself"

"You have the power to turn every seemingly negative situation into something good and positive. But let me caution you, Bantam, sometimes this will take a long time, so you will need to develop and practice patience. Be optimistic. I know for sure that you can do it, the seeds of greatness are within you."

"But Foster," said Bantam, "is there more reason for me being here than knowing myself and growing into the best tree that I can be?"

"Yes, Bantam, there is. Our purpose is to be for others. To do that, you must first take the gift of life you have and grow and develop yourself. Then, in your own chosen way, make a gift of yourself to others."

"Foster," said Bantam, "you are so wise. Please tell me about some of the experiences of your life so that I might learn from you."

Foster looked into Bantam's little eyes and then broke into a warm tender smile. Foster was very happy that young Bantam asked him to share some of the experiences of his life. So he began to open his heartwood to Bantam. "Bantam," said Foster, "look into my heartwood and I'll tell you about my life."

With the help of a little breeze, Bantam bent over Foster's stump and gazed into his heartwood. Foster explained that each ring on his stump stood for one year of his life. So Bantam followed his story by counting Foster's rings.

"I grew rapidly the first ten years of my life," said Foster. "You can tell that from my wide growth rings. I had plenty of sunshine and water. My roots found their way into the rich soil as the rest of me grew toward the sun. Knowing your roots, Bantam, will help you grow, no matter what befalls you."

"But then something began to happen to me and my growth slowed. I was confused for the next several years because each year I seemed to grow less than the year before. Then one day some loggers came through and thinned out some of the trees close to me, all except one that is. The next year I began growing faster again. As I looked back at that period I learned an important lesson, Bantam, and that is to stick it out because things will get better. That is when I first learned about patience."

"In Your Own Chosen Way, Make A Gift Of Yourself To Others"

"For the next seven years," continued Foster, "I grew and grew and grew. I branched out. I really began being for others as I discovered the depths of my roots. I felt good about myself. I was excited about living. I kept the soil from washing away. I produced oxygen for animals and humans to breathe. Birds found shelter in my branches. People found peace and shade as they leaned up against my trunk."

"If you look closer at my heartwood, Bantam, you'll see that something happened to me during my twenty-first year. A person from a nearby camping party chopped away at my side, for no good reason, with a sharp hatchet. I had done them no harm at all and what did I get......my side cut open. But rather than feeling sorry for myself I got on with my life and continued to grow. Still it took about seven years before I completely healed over. From that experience I learned that time heals."

"Just as I got over that attack to my side I went into a long depression. You see, Bantam," said Foster, "a severe dry spell struck. For three years I hardly had any water. It was a long dry spell. You can tell this because my growth rings are so close together. I looked to my roots for help through this period. I knew if I could hang on that things would get better and I would begin to grow again."

"Let me tell you, Bantam, this time I was really put to the test. Just when I thought things couldn't get any worse, they did. Because of the terribly dry conditions a cigarette butt from a careless smoker ignited the ground cover. The high winds fanned the fire so fast that only one side of my trunk was burned. The firefighters responded quickly and soon had the fire under control. But it was two more weeks before the rains came and the drought was over. You can see, Bantam, that it took about five years before I recovered from my burns."

Bantam looked at Foster and asked, "Why didn't you give up when all this happened to you?"

"I had a dream. I believed that I could make a difference, that I could make a better world for both those around me and for those who were to come after me," said Foster. "Knowing now, that I could live through tough times and grow again made me that much stronger and more determined."

"Believe In Yourself"

"For the next twenty-one years I lived a very normal life. I developed a beautiful relationship with my friend, Victoria. We grew close. Our branches actually grew together. We were almost like one. In the spring time we frolicked together as all of nature came alive again. During the long summer months we soaked up the sun. In the fall we enjoyed the beautiful colors around us. Winter was our time to be still and speak to each other in silence. But we always looked forward to spring. That was our chance to start to grow again. I loved Victoria."

"But then it happened, in the spring of the year, the most trying time of my entire life. The air became still, not a leaf moved. The birds and animals were silent and nowhere to be seen. The sky blackened. I heard a roar and saw debris flying through the air. A terrible, devastating, storm came up. It shook me to the ends of my roots. It ripped my crown off and just that fast, it disappeared. But right behind the storm came the lightning."

"Yes, Bantam, you guessed it, a bolt of lightning struck me and followed my trunk down to the ground, opening up my side. I really thought this was the end for me. I stood there shaking, the top of me completely removed, my side split open. Then the storm passed and I looked around to see if there was any other damage."

"I couldn't believe it was possible, I just didn't think it was true. My dear companion Victoria, had been taken away from me. The storm had uprooted her and just took her away. To me, Victoria was the greatest tree that ever lived. We had many long talks together and shared so much with each other. I cried. It was hard for me to think about living without her. Remember, Bantam, it's ok to cry when you lose a loved one."

"Then I got angry because Victoria had been snatched from me. And yes, it's ok to be angry for a time too! Next my anger gave way to depression."

"It's Ok To Cry..."

"It's Ok To Be
Angry, For A Time"

"Finally, one day after a gentle rain had stopped, I raised my head. Stretched across the sky was a rainbow, my symbol of hope. I realized I was richer for having known Victoria."

"I asked myself if I was satisfied with my life. I thought about it for some time. Then I decided, no I'm not satisfied with my life, I want to continue to live and to be more for others, to really love others, to laugh more."

"Listen To That
Silent Voice Guiding
You From Within"

"And Bantam," said Foster, "that will to live, that hope for a better world, and the ability to laugh are keys to the healing process and continued growth. I was a pitiful sight with my crown gone and my side split open. But I had an overpowering will to live and I had a dream, a purpose. Listening to that silent voice within, I once again began growing toward the sun."

"Choose Life"

"Find Peace"

"As time went on I thought more and more about the many positive things that Victoria and I shared together. I always missed Victoria but my loneliness eventually gave way to fond, loving memories that brought me great joy, strength and peace. In time these memories put a smile back on my face. And in her silence I knew that Victoria was still with me. I came to understand that she was a gift and it was now up to me to carry on my life and to also be a gift. To be a positive ray of hope to others, but in my own special way."

"This is not to say that progress wasn't slow, Bantam," said Foster. "My earlier hurts had all healed and were known only to me. I kept them deep within my heartwood. Up until this time in my life no one could see the hurt I suffered."

"Now things were different. I was ugly and would be scarred for the rest of my life. But that inner strength came through to me again. Deep inside I knew that life was still good. That my job was still to be the best tree that I can be with what I had, even if my crown had been taken away."

"Be The Best
That You Can Be
With What You Have"

"It wasn't but a couple months after the crippling storm left me hurting so bad that I got struck again. You see, some people came along, putting in wooden fence posts and stringing barbed wire. And wouldn't you know, when they came past me, they didn't put in a fence post. They just stapled the barbed wire to my side."

"But Bantam, by this time I had a deep desire to live. I was determined to continue to live, grow, experience life and be a gift even though I was scarred and looked ugly. Every year I added another growth ring. I began to overcome the barb in my side. I grew right around it and covered it up."

"Years later a work party came along. I heard them talking excitedly. They were going to make a park out of the area and were removing the barbed wire fence. When they came to me and saw how I just grew around the barbed wire they stood back, amazed. Knowing they couldn't possibly remove the staple, they just cut the wire off and left the rest of it inside me. That was just fine with me. I had grown used to it now and I had it locked within my heartwood. In time I would have it buried deep inside me, just like my other hurts. It would be known only to me. No one else would ever know about it. No one except you, Bantam."

"As the years passed I continued to grow. I added a new ring each year. And every year, more and more visitors came through the park. And I became quite well known. I became the doorway to the park. I was a survivor of the terrible storm. Eventually my side grew closed again. But I still had a hollow shaft inside me from that fierce bolt of lightning."

"Remember, Bantam, when I told you that you have the power to turn every seemingly negative situation into something good and positive? Well, here's a good example. That hollowness inside me now became a home for a family of chipmunks. And the chipmunks attracted even more visitors to the park. People loved to sit in my shade, look up at me and watch the chipmunks scamper over my branches, down my trunk and around my base. And the birds would come and entertain with their beautiful songs."

"Sometimes I watched people as they walked by. Some of them would look up at me and stop. They'd step back a bit. They'd walk around me, and look closely at me. Some even touched my wrinkled bark. Then I'd hear them comment, 'Oh, what a beautiful tree!'"

"When this first started to happen, I just didn't believe them. You see, Bantam, I thought I was still ugly, crippled, deformed and now old. But I kept hearing people say that I was beautiful. And that got me looking at myself again. By taking the time to look inside I finally discovered how special and unique I really was. I was the best tree that I could be with what I had. I learned that it was the very hardships of life that actually created my beauty. I began to think well of myself again. And that's very important, Bantam."

"Be Easy On Yourself"

"I stood for many more years in the park. I grew toward the sun. At night I reached for the moon and the stars as the fireflies danced among my branches. I was home for the chipmunks and a shelter for the birds. I liked who I was and where I was. I enjoyed greeting all the visitors at the entrance to the park."

"I knew I was getting on in years even though I still thought young, still looked with enthusiasm toward the future and still had dreams. I knew someday I would leave this park. But I even looked forward to that and dreamed about what I might become after I left the park."

"One day a park worker came along and planted a tiny seedling next to me. And that, Bantam, was you! I was so happy when you came, Bantam, and I watched over you carefully. I so enjoyed sharing those early years with you, all the time knowing I would be leaving soon. And yet it would be my leaving that would in time release more energy for you to grow."

"...A Celebration
Of A Life Lived"

"It was after you got a good start, Bantam, that the loggers came to celebrate my leaving. It was a celebration of a life lived, and that's how it should be. All the park workers and many visitors came to see me that day. The loggers layed me gently down. Then they raised my main trunk up onto a big truck for a ride to the sawmill. After arriving at the sawmill, I was changed into lumber and then made into beautiful doors. Where once I was a single doorway to a beautiful park, I now became many doorways to many beautiful passages."

"And the rest of me......they sent to the paper mill where I was changed into paper, paper much like this. And on this paper is written the same story that was once only written in my growth rings. So you see, Bantam, I really didn't die, I just changed forms and I keep on giving."

"Have heartwood, Bantam. Be easy on yourself. Find peace. Love yourself and then love others. Rejoice and be glad with your life. Follow that silent voice within and be a gift to others. You are an active participant in the creation of this world. Remember your roots and grow toward the sun. Think well of yourself and be optimistic. Go now and enjoy the rest of your life."

"You Are An Active Participant In The Creation Of This World"

"Go Now And Enjoy
The Rest Of Your Life"